E
Radunsky

YUBA COUNTY LIBRARY
MARYSVILLE, CA

VIKING Published by the Penguin Group
Penguin Putnam Books for Young Readers, 345 Hudson Street, New York, New York 10014, U.S.A.
Penguin Books Ltd, Registered Offices: Harmondsworth, Middlesex, England
First published in 2002 by Viking, a division of Penguin Putnam Books for Young Readers.
10  9  8  7  6  5  4  3  2  1
Copyright © Vladimir Radunsky, 2002.  All rights reserved.  Book design by Vladimir Radunsky. Prepress by B-Side Studio Grafico, Rome.
Library of Congress Cataloging-in-Publication Data
Radunsky, Vladimir    Ten / by Vladimir Radunsky    p. cm.    ISBN 0-670-03563-7
[1. Armadillos—Fiction. 2. Babies—Fiction. 3. Pregnancy—Fiction.]  I. Title.   PZ7.R1226 Te 2002    2002002051
Set in FuturaExtrabold   Printed in Hong Kong                                        [Fic]—dc21

# Before the Story Begins

I will tell you a story about an armadillo. Or perhaps I should say two armadillos.

No, that's not right either. I'd better start from the very beginning.

Do you know what an armadillo looks like?

## The Armadillo
(naked, after taking a bath)

tail

shell

feet

claws

eyes

ears

nose

Of course, when armadillos go for a walk or to see a friend, they dress up.
They are very fond of fine clothes.

## First,

they put on nice ear socks. Always clean. Always in bright colors.

## Second,

a well brought up armadillo never leaves home without a proper tail stocking.

## Third,

they always, always paint their noses, usually blue (nobody knows why).

## Fourth,

they always wear pretty dresses or elegant suits.

## Fifth,

armadillos usually walk on all four legs, but sometimes they walk on two, like you and me. It all depends on their mood. Most of the time they are in a very good mood.

# What should I call this story? Hmm . . . I know! I will call it . . .

YUBA COUNTY LIBRARY
MARYSVILLE, CA

# 10

## (ten)

# a wonderful story

**The story and pictures will be mine.**

that's me, Vladimir Radunsky

**Viking**

# The Story Begins

Here is the town where Mr. and Mrs. Armadillo live.

They just got married, and they are crazy about each other.

Villa Armadillo

All day long they play. First, Mrs. Armadillo chases

Mr. Armadillo. Then, when she gets tired, they switch.

And so forth and so on.

But when both are tired, they sit down on a bench and say

hello to every armadillo passing by.

Mr. and Mrs. Armadillo are very friendly.

# Mr. and Mrs. Armadillo Dream

Mr. and Mrs. Armadillo also like to sit on the couch and hug.
First, Mrs. Armadillo hugs Mr. Armadillo. Then, when she
gets tired, Mr. Armadillo hugs Mrs. Armadillo.

And so forth and so on.

And what are their names?

Mr. Armadillo's is . . . hmm . . .

**Alfred? Aaron?
Amos? Augustin?**

No, definitely not

**Augustin** . . . Oh, I have

forgotten his name.

And Mrs. Armadillo? Her name is . . . hmm . . . **Amanda? Agatha? Alberta . . . ?** I don't remember.

Anyway they were very happy.

But they were not totally happy, because they did not have any children. And without children their happiness was not complete.

Mr. Armadillo used to say, "If I have a daughter, I will name her **Binky** or **Zoe** or **Chloe.** Or maybe **Muffy?** Yes, **Muffy.**"

And Mrs. Armadillo used to dream, "If I had a son, I would name him **Benjamin** or **Algernon** or **Edward.** Or maybe **Pooky?** Yes, **Pooky.** I like **Pooky** very much."

## One Morning

One morning after coffee, Mr. Armadillo, as usual, called to Mrs. Armadillo, "Catch me!"
"No, I can't," said Mrs. Armadillo. "Look how big my belly is. I think I am going to have a baby."
"Oh, my," said Mr. Armadillo.

## After Some Time

The belly was getting bigger and bigger. Mr. Armadillo kept hugging the belly and asking, "How do you feel, Mrs. Armadillo?"
"I am fine, thank you."

"Oh, Mrs. Armadillo.
Your belly. . . How do you
feel, Mrs. Armadillo?"
"Thank you,
I am fine."

"Ooh, you are huge!
How do you feel,
Mrs. Armadillo?"
"I am fine, thank you."

# The Baby's on the Way!

"Aaaaaaaah . . . Wake up, Mr. Armadillo! We must rush to the
hospital." Mr. Armadillo jumped behind the wheel and they sped
off. No, they flew to the hospital. The night was very dark, and
the wind was blowing hard in their faces.

# At the Hospital

"You are going to be fine," said Dr. Armadillo. "Just fine."
"Hello Pooky, my boy . . . Do I see a Muffy? **Two?**
**Three-e-e??** No, stop, that's enough! **Four? Five?**
Help, I can't count that high! **Six! Seven!!** Call the
doctor! No, I am the doctor. **NURSE! HELP! Eight!**
**Nine! Ten!** Holy Armadillo, **10!**"

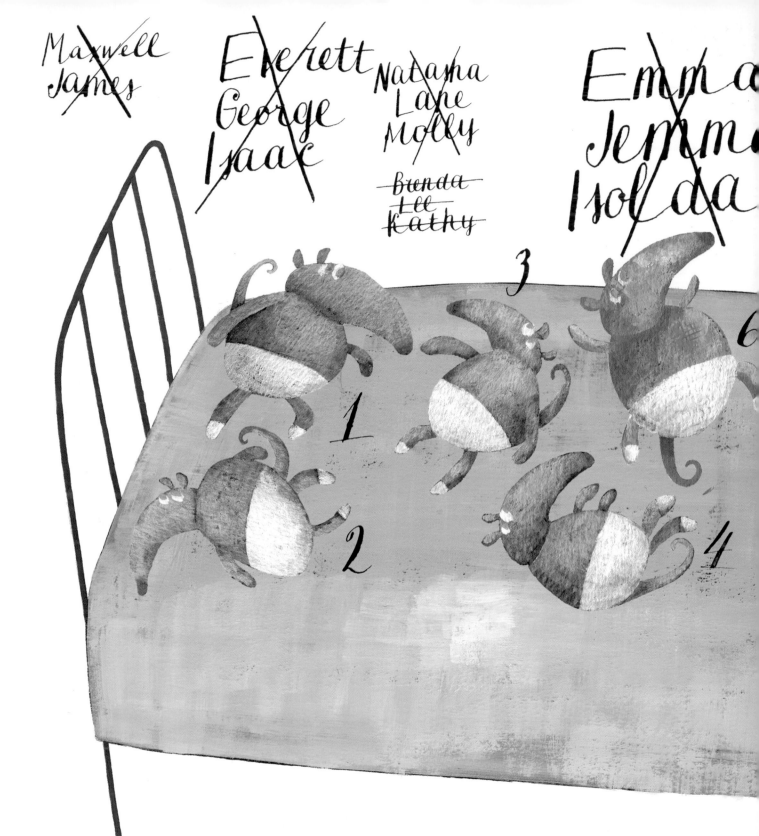

"Oh, Mr. Armadillo, dear. I am the happiest armadillo in the world!
But what are we going to do? We have not decided on any names."
"Oh, very well. We'll call them: **One**, **Two** (she looks like me,
by the way), **Three**, **Four**, **Five**, **Six** (hmm, a pink one!

**No matter, we'll love him anyway),** **Seven** **(I think he has your beautiful eyes),** **Eight, Nine,** **and** **Ten.** **Yes.** **One, Two, Three, Four, Five, Six** **(what a beautiful shade), Seven, Eight, Nine, Ten.** **Perfect names. I am so happy."**

# The Relatives Came

Grandma and Grandpa Armadillo came first.
Grandma brought 10 potties. "What if they all need to go potty at the same time?" she said. And Grandpa brought 10 baseball caps. Grandpa likes baseball. But please don't ask me which team. I don't remember. It does not matter, because they were so happy.

# More Gifts

Then Mrs. Armadillo's brother came. His name was Elmer, Uncle Elmer. He brought 10 tutus. "All my life I wanted to be a ballerina," said Uncle Elmer. "But Grandpa Armadillo wanted me to play baseball. Today, I feel like dancing!" He was so happy.

# And More Gifts

Then Mr. and Mrs. Armadillo's sister-in-law (Uncle Elmer's wife) arrived. "Ten! Ten pets! Every armadillo child needs a pet. We armadillos love animals!" she yelled. She was so happy.

What a noise they all made, especially the cows. They were mooing, "Milk, milk, babies need milk." But everybody was so happy.